The Muffletumps

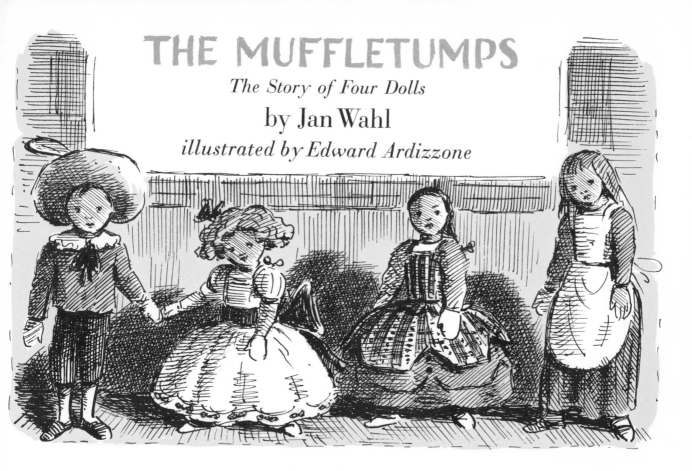

THE MUFFLETUMPS

The Story of Four Dolls

by Jan Wahl

illustrated by Edward Ardizzone

Holt, Rinehart & Winston / New York Chicago San Francisco

Books by Jan Wahl

The Muffletumps

Cabbage Moon

Hello, Elephant

The Howards Go Sledding

Shirley Kerruish, they are for you.

Every summer, the Bediggian family piled things
into the auto and drove off to Pear Lake—
leaving their big house
empty
and alone.

Up in the attic there were large trunks from
long ago.

Muffle!

Thump!

Mysterious noises came from the trunks!

The lids would open just as the Bediggians

disappeared.

Mysterious, brown sounds!

Soft and rustling!

Down from the attic they step in a row!

Edward, who has a hat,

and Henrietta,
who is the oldest and
has left behind her gloves
and doesn't care,

Elsie, who is humming to herself,

and last of all Maud,

who walks straight as a stick

until her joints start to unbend.

When the people family go, then
the Muffletumps take over.
The house is theirs.
They see that the clocks are wound,
that the ceiling doesn't leak much,
and with pails and mops they scrub the floors.

They walked once around from one end slowly
to the other, for the trunks were very stuffy.

At the beginning, they were always sewing

new strings on their bonnets—

mending—

and pressing out the ruffles on their hems.

Except for Edward. He made up poems.

One of them was,

> *Bumblebee,*
> *Thinking of honey,*
> *Wish you'd bring us*
> *A lot of money.*

It was a pretty good poem.

Elsie took away the note which read,

STOP THE MILK,

putting in one that said,

START THE MILK AGEN.

Henrietta was often burning
a terrific number of cakes.
Then she had to dry her tears with her apron.

They had to mend the dishes they broke.

They put out pans of milk for the neighborhood
dogs
Marianne and Loo, and their friends.

Elsie looked beautiful in Mrs. Bediggian's
dressing gown.

I *believe* that is Elsie.

Edward and Maud were not very good at cards.

It was Maud
who liked to look wistfully out at
the tulip tree.
She didn't know why.
Maybe she wanted to climb it.

Here are Maud and Henrietta and Elsie and
Edward,

trying to read.

But Henrietta, the cook, is the only one

who really can.

They all wished THEY might skip on the lawn.

In the evenings, with the curtains shut,
Elsie played the upright piano.
Maud and Henrietta took turns dancing with Edward.

Sometimes they got dressed up as Indians.

At night, when everybody else was snoozing,
they would walk in their back yard
holding candles to see with.

One day the postman came with a package.

He was surprised to see a little wood hand

reach out for it.

He decided he was dreaming.

They SHOULD have put the package
away in a closet.

However, Edward had to look inside.

It was a box of nice-smelling lavender soap.

They each took a cake of soap.

Chewing it made them sleepy.

Henrietta got sick from her cake of soap.

She had to stay in bed.

Even as a nurse, Maud loved to wear too many

orange and purple ribbons.

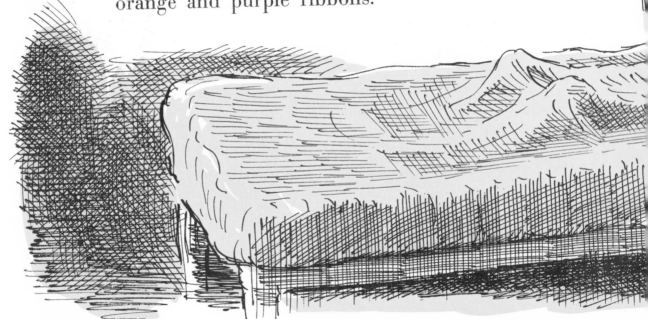

Because none of the others knew how to cook,

Edward served them crackers.

When Henrietta got well again
she fixed them a *lot* of
fried eggs and Gooseberries Henrietta.
These were better than crackers.

And then—so soon?

They heard the Bediggians' auto

crunch-crunching

up the drive. . . .

The Muffletumps fled upstairs.

Elsie murmured,

"Goodbye, piano dear,"

just before the front door opened.

Mrs. Bediggian found

a couple of toasted muffins burning.

Every year it was SOMETHING.

Henrietta climbed in first.

They felt their tired limbs grow stiff.

Summer was over;

it was time to sleep again.

A native of Ohio, Jan Wahl attended Cornell University and the University of Michigan, where he was the recipient of the Avery Hopwood Award in fiction in 1955. Mr. Wahl also spent a year in Denmark, studying Scandinavian films and folk literature. The author of THE HOWARDS GO SLEDDING, HELLO, ELEPHANT, and CABBAGE MOON, Mr. Wahl now lives in Brooklyn, where he collects old movies and antique toys.

Edward Ardizzone, who illustrated HELLO, ELEPHANT, also by Jan Wahl, was born in Indochina, but grew up in England, where he still lives. He began drawing as a pupil in an English public school and continued to pursue his study of art in the evenings at the Westminster School in London, while working as a clerk. In 1940, Mr. Ardizzone was appointed official war artist for England. He is the distinguished illustrator of over one hundred books for adults and children.